Pemba
SHERPA

By Olga Cossi

Illustrated by Gary Bernard

ODYSSEY BOOKS

Published 2009 by Odyssey Books, a division of The Ciletti Publishing Group, Inc.

Text copyright © 2009 Olga Cossi

Illustrations copyright © 2009 Gary Bernard

Printed in Korea by Pacifica Communications. All rights reserved. Except as permitted under the United States Copyright Act, no part of this publication may be reproduced or distributed in any form or by any means or stored in a database or retrieval system without prior written permission from the publisher.

Library of Congress Cataloging-in-Publication Data is on file with the publisher.

Send all inquiries to:

Odyssey Books

463 Main St. Suite 200

Longmont, Colorado 80501

ISBN: 978-0-9768655-8-2

18918

First Edition

1 2 3 4 5 6 7 8 9 10

Dedicated to

Pemba Doma Sherpa,

the first Nepali woman

to summit Mount Everest

via the North Face.

Today, I am a nyuny pa, which in Tibet means that I am an old man. But there was a time when I was young like you who are reading my story. I lived in the Sherpa village of Khumjung, in the foothills of the Himalayan mountains of Nepal. From my village I could see Mount Everest, which reaches to the great height of 29,035 feet, making it the highest mountain peak in the world.

I am a Sherpa. My ancestors came from Tibet. Sherpas are world famous for their work as porters and guides. We lead the climbers and trekkers who try to reach the snowcapped peaks of the Himalayas.

Like every other schoolchild in Khumjung, I dreamed of becoming the best porter and guide in all of Nepal. My younger sister Yang Ki wanted to be a porter, too. But, at that time, girls were not allowed to train for this work. I knew this, and so did Yang Ki. I can close my eyes and remember, just like I am there, the day that would change our lives forever. . . .

I am once again a schoolboy. This morning, just like every morning, I have to get up very early to walk down past Jorsale to get a load of firewood for the stove in the classroom. Each student brings wood to school during the warmer months. Without the heat from the stove, we would not be able to sit and study during the long winter months when snow covers the mountain.

This morning my little sister, Yang Ki, wakes up early, too. She wants to gather wood with me.

"You are too little to carry wood," I tell her. "Go back to bed."

Yang Ki does not listen. She looks at me with calm eyes and says, "I want to carry wood so when I am bigger I will be strong enough to be a porter. I want to talk with people on the trail and learn to speak English, and then I can be a guide."

I laugh at her. "You are a girl! Girls cannot be guides!"

Yang Ki does not laugh. She just looks at me and says, "I am a Sherpa, just like you."

"You are a girl, and you are only seven years old," I tell her. "If you want to carry wood, carry it to Mother's stove so she can make lentil soup and have hot tea ready for me when I come home from school."

Yang Ki's eyes do not leave me as I wrap my head in a yak wool scarf (rumal) and put on my jacket and shoes. I pick up my tumpline (namlo) and the basket that I use to carry heavy burdens. The tumpline is a headband that helps support the loads we carry in the basket on our backs. Then I am on my way.

The sun is not up as I start down the long, steep trail to Jorsale where my father is cutting wood. It takes almost three hours to run down, fill my basket, and carry it back up to school before classes start at nine o'clock.

When I reach the steepest, narrowest part of the trail, I hear a sound behind me. It is probably Yang Ki following me. I wait for her to catch up.

"Go back! You cannot come with me!" I shout at her.

Yang Ki does not move.

"Go back!" I repeat angrily. "It is too far for me to take you home!"

Yang Ki shakes her head and says, "No!"

I am so angry that I think of throwing a stone at her. But she is my little sister, and I cannot do that.

"The Yeti will get you," I tell Yang Ki, hoping to scare her.

The Yeti is our legendary snowman. His footprints have been seen not far from here.

Yang Ki shows no fear. I am not surprised.

I shrug my shoulders and start running again. I hurry even faster than before. If Yang Ki loses sight of me, she may become discouraged and turn back.

The trail drops sharply and my feet fly over the rocks. Suddenly as I round a turn, a landslide breaks loose from the high bank. It thunders past me toward the steep canyon far below.

I am running too fast. I cannot stop. My feet hit the loose rocks. I am caught in the landslide. I fall headlong toward the edge of the canyon.

My fingers claw the earth. It is no use. The force of the landslide carries me with it.

What can I do? I see a tree root. I lunge for it and hang on. I grind to a stop inches from the edge.

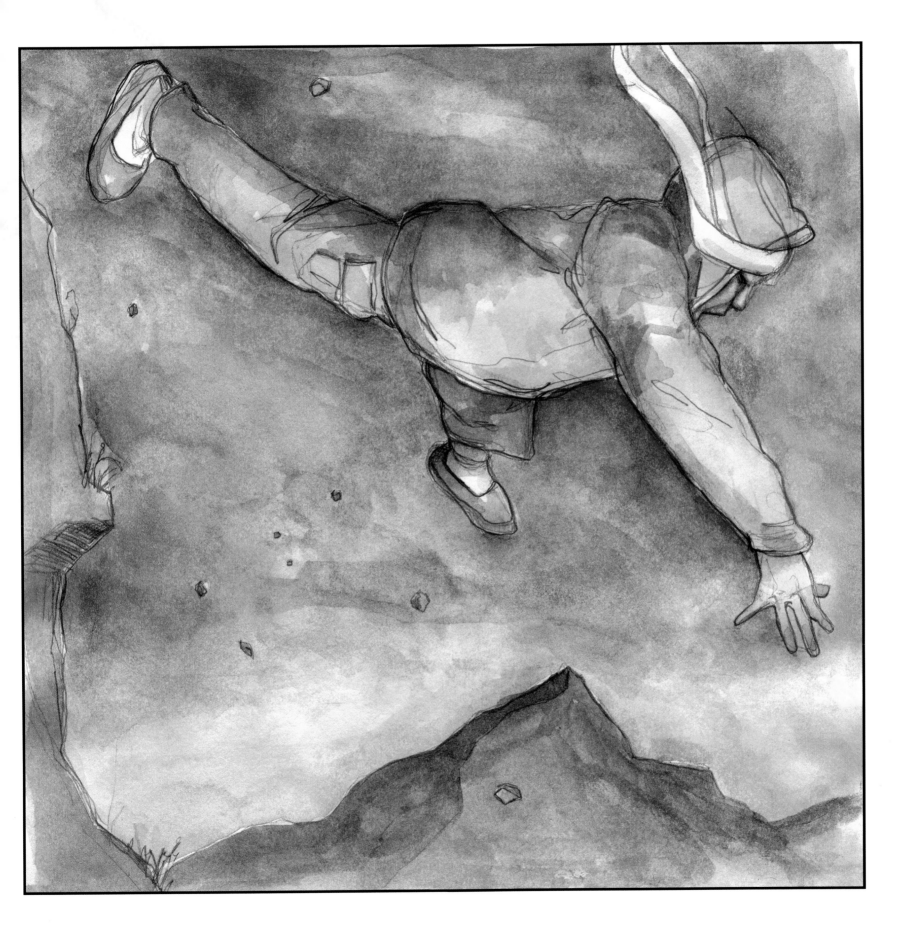

My heart drums in my chest. I am afraid to shout. My voice may start a new landslide and take me with it. I am afraid to look down. I stay perfectly still and wait for my heartbeat to slow down.

As soon as my breath returns, I look up. Yang Ki is standing beside the trail above me. I close my eyes to hold back the tears. When I open them again, she is not there.

It seems like forever before Yang Ki comes back. She is dragging a long bamboo pole. It looks green and fresh. How did she cut it, I wonder?

I do not wonder for long. My arms are aching from holding the root. My strength is giving out. I will have to let go very soon.

Yang Ki takes one step down the bank where the landslide began. Then another step. Then another. Slowly, carefully, she makes her way to a large tree. She braces herself against the trunk. She pushes the bamboo pole toward me. I watch it come closer . . . closer . . . at last, it is within reach.

I look up at Yang Ki. Our eyes meet. We both know that my life is in her hands. Is she strong enough to hold her end of the pole while I pull myself up?

There is no time to think of what might happen if she lets go. I reach quickly for the pole. My fingers grip its smooth greenness and hold fast. I sink my fingernails into it to keep from slipping.

Yang Ki holds the narrow end of the bamboo with both hands. I pull on the other end, testing to see if she can stand my weight when I start to climb. She does not waver. I pull harder. Still she does not let the pole slip in her hands. I feel her strength and must trust it.

My eyes meet Yang Ki's once more. She is ready. I take a deep breath and make my move.

In an instant, I have both hands on the pole and am pulling myself up. My feet scramble trying to get a foothold in the sliding earth. The sound of rocks crashing below echoes through the canyon. I keep my eyes on Yang Ki and pull harder. She does not waver. Her thin arms are like steel bands holding the pole in place.

I work my way upward, hand over hand. At last, I reach the tree where she is braced. I wrap my arm around the trunk and pull myself to safety. We let go of the pole. We watch silently as it slithers away and disappears down the canyon.

For a moment, we rest against the tree. Then Yang Ki pulls my tumpline and basket free from the brush where they are snagged. After we catch our breath, I try to stand. Only then do I feel the pain in my ankle. Again I try to stand, but the pain makes me weak. I slump to the ground and examine my ankle. It is swollen and stiff. How will I get my load of firewood for school, I wonder?

Yang Ki sees my pain and knows what to do. "Come quickly," she says. "There is a spring just up the trail where the bamboo grows. The water is like ice. It will stop the swelling."

We have gone only a short distance when we meet a group of porters carrying loads down the steep trail. "Namaste," they say as they rest on their walking sticks. Yang Ki and I return the traditional greeting.

I tell them about the landslide and how Yang Ki just rescued me. They are proud of my little sister and tell me so. They slip off their tumplines and baskets and go to repair the trail to make it passable before they attempt to go farther.

Yang Ki helps me as I limp to the spring around the next bend. I plunge my foot into the icy pool formed by a natural dam of rocks. The water is so cold that it hurts worse than the sprain. I grit my teeth and turn to thank Yang Ki. She is gone! So are my tumpline and basket. I feel very helpless. There is nothing I can do but wait there with my foot turning numb.

It is a long time before Yang Ki comes back. She is wearing my tumpline on her forehead and carrying a load of firewood in my basket on her back.

I am proud and angry at the same time. What will my friends at school say when they know that my seven-year-old little sister carried my load of firewood for me?

I do not have time to think about it. Yang Ki reaches my side and rests on the tree branch she is using for a walking stick.

"I cannot let you carry my firewood for me!" I sputter.

Yang Ki looks at me with big eyes and says nothing. She turns and starts walking up the trail.

"I said you cannot carry my firewood for me!" I shout after her.

Yang Ki answers without looking back. "I am going to carry it anyway. Today, I am *your* porter . . . and *your* guide."

"No!" I object, but Yang Ki keeps right on walking.

There is nothing I can do but follow her. Oh, how it hurts when I take the first step! I try to ignore the pain and hobble after Yang Ki. She cannot do this to me. She is my little sister and should obey me, I tell myself.

At first I shout these words at Yang Ki. I might as well be talking to the cuckoo birds (kufi) for all the good it does. I can tell that nothing is going to stop her.

It takes a long time to walk up the steep trail to Khumjung. In spite of the load she is carrying, Yang Ki keeps well ahead of me, making certain that I do not get close enough to snatch the firewood from her.

By the time we reach the school, I am very tired and very proud of my little sister. I no longer care what my friends think as they see her carry firewood for me. The tale of my sister's bravery quickly spreads through our village, and then throughout the land. After that, I never doubted that Yang Ki would become a guide.

All of this happened many years ago. Today I am a nyuny pa. My heart swells with pride when I think of Yang Ki. Girls were once thought to be too weak or fragile to work as porters and guides. But my little sister, with her enormous courage, changed that thinking.

Today, women are among the most famous Sherpas in the world. Yang Ki taught us that girls, even little girls, could be brave and strong, with a heart big enough to be Sherpa.

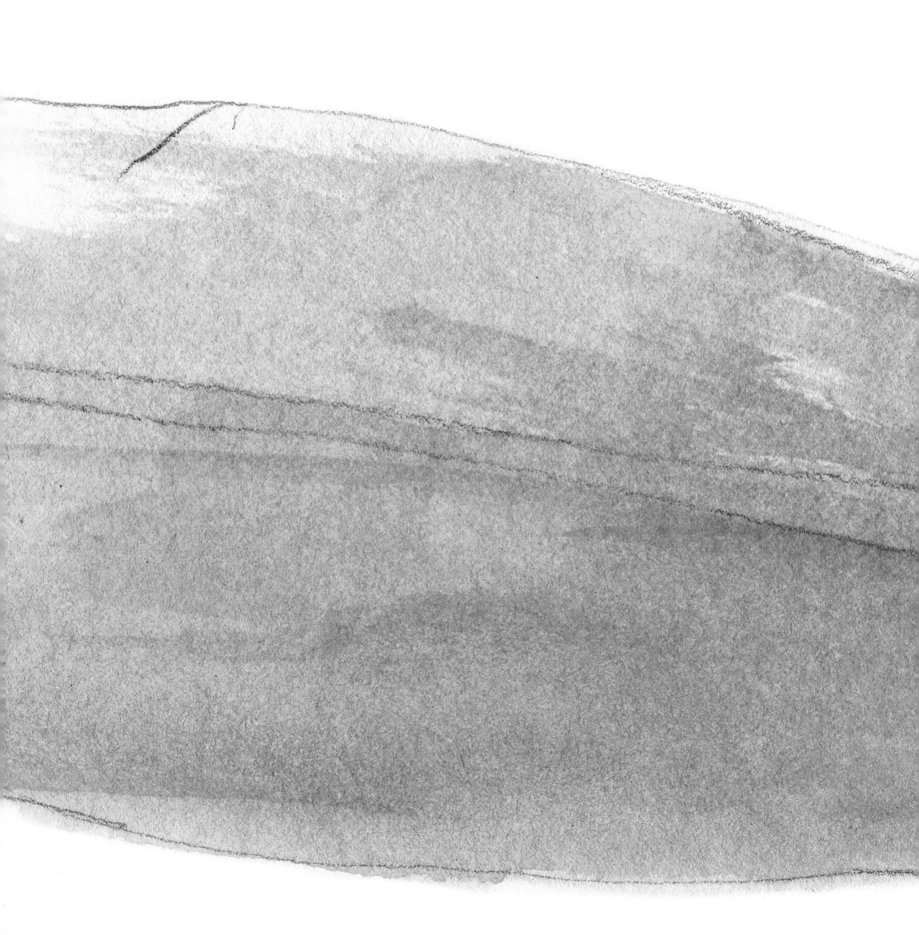

The End

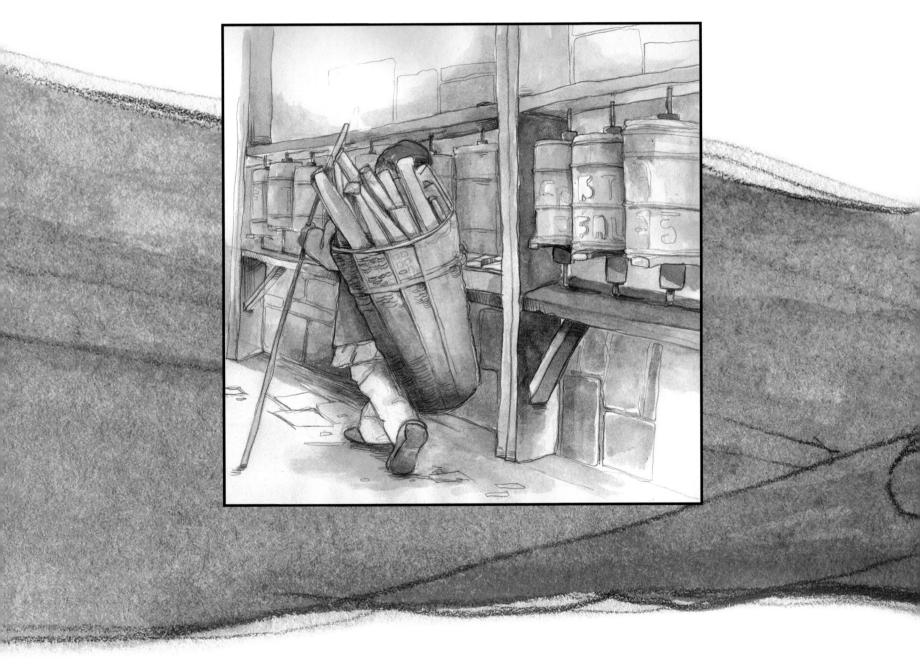